SEA EXPLORERS

Volume 3

Rick Steber—Writing

Don Gray—Illustrations

Printed in the West
by
Maverick Publications

ISBN 0-945134-77-0

BONANZA PUBLISHING • PRINEVILLE, OREGON

America has been discovered many times. Historians believe the first discovery was made between 15,000 and 40,000 years ago by Mongoloids who crossed a land and ice bridge between northern Asia and North America. These people spread over the continent and after thousands of years they developed diverse languages and living habits depending on the bounty of Mother Nature in their region.

Later discoveries are credited to Norsemen, who are believed to have landed on the northeast coast. There is also evidence Irish monks crossed the Atlantic in rawhide boats. Artifacts found in Mexico suggest Egyptian influence. Documents of the Sung Dynasty from 458 A.D. give details of a Buddhist priest who sailed to the New World and returned to China. But the most famous discovery was credited to Christopher Columbus in 1492.

The Pacific Northwest was one of the last places to be discovered by the Europeans. As explorers searched along the Pacific coast for the Northwest Passage that would return them to the Atlantic Ocean, they stumbled upon a vast land inhabited by many diverse tribes of native people. This story of *Sea Explorers* chronicles the voyages of these courageous sailors who came to the far corner of the world in search of trade and exploration.

Shortly after the first voyage by Christopher Columbus to North America the world was divided by papal decree between Spain and Portugal. The dividing line gave Spain the newly discovered land to the west and Portugal everything to the east. If their paths overlapped, ownership was to be determined by priority of discovery.

The first European to sight the Pacific Ocean was Vasco Nunez de Balboa in 1513. From a hilltop at the Isthmus of Panama he looked out over a vast body of water and claimed it and all the land the waters broke upon in the name of Spain.

Balboa learned from natives of the existence of neighboring civilizations rich in gold, silver and jewelry. Francisco Hernandez de Cordoba was sent to plunder the Yucatan Peninsula, home of the Mayas; Hernando Cortes marched into Mexico to loot and destroy the ancient Aztec culture.

Ferdinand Magellan, flying the flag of Spain, sailed around the tip of South America in 1520 into a great, calm sea. He named it the Pacific Ocean. With the gates now opened other Spaniards rounded Cape Horn to search for the fabled Northwest Passage.

Juan Rodriguez Cabrillo, sent to find this passage, explored the coast of California to a point north of San Francisco Bay where he became sick and died. His pilot, Bartolome Ferrelo, assumed command. The expedition continued northward and the men may have been the first Europeans to see the coast of Oregon. Cape Ferrelo, located along the Oregon-California border, was named in honor of this expedition.

Sir Francis Drake, the most daring and dashing of all pirates, departed from his home port of Plymouth, England in 1577. He sailed for the Pacific and after rounding Cape Horn began slipping into Spanish ports, one after another, stripping them of their riches. Passing ships were chased down, boarded and their crews forced to walk the plank.

It was claimed that on board Drake's small vessel, the *Golden Hind*, was a treasure of not less than 26 tons of silver bars, 80 pounds of pure gold and 13 chests overflowing with pearls, emeralds and other precious stones. The vessel became so heavy with plunder that a part of the cargo, including silks and spices from the Orient, had to be thrown overboard.

Rather than returning home the way they had come, and running the gauntlet of war ships across the Spanish Main, Drake decided to sail northward in the hope of discovering the Northwest Passage. He passed along the Oregon coast and reported running into cold weather at a latitude of 48° north (near Vancouver Island), weather so cold the rigging was covered with ice and the crew, fresh from the tropics, pleaded with Drake to turn back.

Reluctantly Drake ordered his ship south. The *Golden Hind*, leaking badly, was forced to put in along the coast for repairs. Some historians believe the harbor was San Francisco Bay while others claim it was Whales Cove on the Oregon coast.

After laying over for more than a month the *Golden Hind* returned to sea. Drake pointed his ship toward the southwest and fourteen months later sailed around the world and into Plymouth Sound, England.

In 1588 the Spanish Armada, a fleet of 130 armed ships carrying 27,000 men, was sent to seize control of the English Channel. The invaders were driven back and nearly all the remaining ships sank during a series of violent storms. After this stinging defeat Spain went through a period of gradual decline. It sought to hold onto Mexico and California by establishing missions and colonies rather than sending out expeditions to seek more land in the North Pacific.

In later years a Greek sailor named Apostolos Valerianos, commonly known as Juan de Fuca, came forward with an account of having been employed by the Viceroy of Mexico to explore for the Northwest Passage. He claimed that his ship, between the latitudes 47° and 48°, had entered a broad inland sea upon which he sailed for twenty days without locating a passageway. Today the Strait of Juan de Fuca bears his name.

By the late 1700s other countries, including Russia, England, France and the United States, began showing interest in the North Pacific. Spain mounted a challenge and in 1774 King

Charles III ordered Juan Perez to sail from Mexico to 60° north. He failed and a second expedition was dispatched.

This expedition included the ship *Santiago* under command of Bruno Heceta and the schooner *Sonora* under Juan Francisco de la Bodega y Quadra. They struck land near the 47th parallel. A boat was dispatched to obtain fresh water and berries if possible because the men were suffering with scurvy. No sooner did the bow touch the shore than natives attacked and killed every man.

Shortly after this tragedy the two vessels were separated by a storm. Quadra continued north and eventually reached the 50th parallel before abandoning the expedition. Heceta turned south and on August 17, 1775, near the 46th parallel, he noted in his log that they were sailing near an opening in the coast from which rushed a current so strong his ship could not enter. Rather than explore the source he was impatient to return to Mexico and missed the opportunity to receive credit for discovering the Great River of the West, the Columbia River.

During the 262 years since Balboa had first gazed on the Pacific Ocean the Spanish government had sent out fifteen expeditions to the North Pacific coast. They had accomplished a superficial exploration, sighting and naming only the prominent landmarks.

THE ENGLISH

In 1776 two British ships, the *Resolution* and the *Discovery*, were fitted for the long voyage to the Pacific. Captain James Cook was directed to search for the fabled Northwest Passage. As an added incentive Parliament offered a reward of 20,000 pounds sterling to any captain who could prove the existence of a waterway between the North Pacific and the Atlantic.

During the voyage the ships came upon a group of islands in the middle of the Pacific. Cook named them the Sandwich Islands (Hawaiian Islands) in honor of the first lord of the admiralty, the Earl of Sandwich.

The ships sailed east but as they neared land a terrific storm rose and made it necessary to run southward with it. At the height of this storm, with the wind howling across the tops of the tall waves, they were swept near a rugged shoreline that appeared out of the mist. Cook named this rocky headland on the Oregon coast Cape Foulweather.

After the storm subsided the expedition sailed northward, catching glimpses of headlands covered by a dark green forest.

Because of blustery weather conditions they sailed past the mouth of the Columbia River and continued north. Cook wrote in his journal that a small round hill gave the appearance of an island and "an opening which flattered us with hope of finding a harbor. On this account I called the point of land to the north of it Cape Flattery." They set a course north and west and missed the entrance to the Strait of Juan de Fuca.

The *Resolution* and *Discovery* dropped anchor along Vancouver Island in Nootka Bay. Immediately a large number of decoratively carved canoes pushed off from the tree-lined shore and made straight for the ships. They were paddled by wild-looking natives who wore brass rings in their noses, tightly woven baskets on their heads and animal skins covering their bodies.

They asked to trade with the white men and offered skins of wolf, fox, bear, deer, martin and sea otter. In return they wanted implements of brass and iron, saying they had salvaged such items from shipwrecks. Two Spanish silver spoons were shown as proof.

It is possible that Spanish galleons could have been blown off course and wrecked along the North Pacific shores. Stories of prehistoric visits by white men were part of many coastal tribes' mythology, including buried treasure on Neahkahnie Mountain, the wreck of the beeswax ship near Nehalem, and the shipwreck at the mouth of the Columbia River that washed ashore two men with white skin and bushy red beards.

Leaving Nootka Bay the two ships followed the Alaska coast until finding the way blocked by Arctic ice. This convinced Cook that the Northwest Passage did not exist and he turned back toward the warm climate of the Sandwich Islands.

On February 14, 1779 at Kealakekua Bay, Captain Cook attempted to retrieve one of the ship's boats stolen by natives and was attacked and clubbed to death before any of his crew could come to his rescue.

The expedition continued west and eventually reached Canton, China. The crew discovered the furs collected along the North Pacific coast were in great demand among the Chinese. Fabulous prices were paid. The crew wanted to immediately procure more furs but Captain Gore ordered the ship's return to England. At home port rumors ran wild that great riches awaited the individuals or companies brave enough to initiate trade between the natives of the North Pacific and the Chinese. The era of the sea trader was dawning.

THE RUSSIANS

In the early 1700s Russia, under the reign of Peter the Great, began looking for ways to expand her borders. Vitus Bering, a Danish naval officer, was commissioned to explore the Siberian coast and the coast of North America.

Bering and his men, suffering greatly from cold and hardships, traveled 2,000 miles by dog team across Russia to eastern Siberia. Here the dogs were used to pull logs from the forest. Lumber was hand-hewn and fitted together to build the ship *Gabriel*. The *Gabriel* was launched July 13, 1728.

After a second voyage the following year, Bering retired. But in 1741 he returned to the sea and set sail on an ill-fated voyage of discovery with two vessels, the *St. Peter* and the *St. Paul.* He explored the coast of Alaska and named the imposing Mt. St. Elias mountain range.

Near the latitude of 60° Bering went ashore to claim the land for Russia. His crew, disabled by scurvy, caused Bering to turn toward home but his ship ran aground and Bering died on an island in the Aleutian chain that today bears his name.

The *St. Paul,* under command of Lieutenant Chirikoff, continued the expedition. In the vicinity of Sitka Sound and in need of fresh water, Chirikoff sent ten of his best men ashore in a small boat. They never returned. Neither did a second party. It was believed they were murdered by the natives.

When this expedition returned to Siberia, bringing with them a few sea otter and seal pelts, the Russians learned the value of the fur trade. In the ensuing years many adventurous Russian traders visited the North American coast where they explored Prince William Sound, Kodiak Island and founded several settlements on the mainland.

In 1806 the Russians at Sitka, Alaska were in need of food. They sailed to California and purchased wheat and farm products, paying the Spaniards with furs. The success of this mission led to the Russian purchase of land on Bodega Bay, California and the building of Fort Ross. This was the southernmost point of Russian influence. It was sold in 1841 to Captain John A. Sutter of Sutter's Fort and the Russians returned north of the 54th parallel.

THE FUR TRADERS

One of the early fur traders was an Englishman, James Hanna. His ship, the *Harmon*, was owned by English merchants, outfitted in China and sailed under Portuguese papers. In one trip between the North Pacific coast and China, a profit of $20,000 was realized from the sale of sea otter pelts.

The following year, 1786, two more English vessels, the *Captain Cook* and the *Experiment*, arrived at Nootka Bay. They gathered a cargo of furs and before departing decided to leave an agent on the coast. Dr. John MacKay, the surgeon on the *Captain Cook*, volunteered to stay and

stockpile furs. He moved into the natives' village and took a wife.

A few months later another Englishman, Captain Charles William Barkley, dropped anchor in Nootka Bay. He was shocked when a canoe came alongside and what appeared to be a dark-skinned native man dressed in a sea otter robe called out in perfect English. He introduced himself as Dr. John MacKay. Captain Barkley offered to return him to civilization but Dr. MacKay declined, saying the diet and the life of the natives suited him.

Two other English ships, under command of Captain John Meares, arrived that same year. The *Nootka* and the *Sea Otter* did not sail together but had arranged to rendezvous in Prince William Sound. Upon his arrival Meares learned that the *Sea Otter* had been there and departed. She and her crew were never heard from again. Meares waited. Winter set in and the *Nootka* became icebound. His crew came down with scurvy.

Meares wrote of that winter: "We continued to see and lament a gradual diminution of our crew. Too often did I find myself called to assist in performing the dreadful office of dragging the dead bodies across the ice to a shallow sepulcher, which with our own hands we had hewn out for them on the shore. The sledge in which we fetched the wood was their hearse and the chasm in the ice their grave."

Spring thaw released the *Nootka.* She sailed for the Orient where Meares changed ships, commanding the *Felice Adventurer* on a return voyage to the coast of North America.

On July 6, 1788 the *Felice Adventurer* reached the entrance of what appeared to be a large bay. Meares wrote: "As we steered in, the water shoaled to nine, eight and seven fathoms, when breakers were seen from the deck, right ahead, and from the masthead, they were observed to extend across the bay, we therefore hauled out, and directed our course to the opposite shore, to see if there was any channel. The name of Cape Disappointment was given the nearby promontory, and the bay obtained the title of Deception Bay."

Meares departed without ever realizing he was at the mouth of the Great River of the West. He sailed north in search of sea otter furs.

One evening six American businessmen met in Boston to form a stock company to actively pursue fur trade with China. The initial capitalization of $50,000 was used to purchase two vessels: the *Columbia Rediviva*, a full-rigged ship of 212 tons; and the *Lady Washington*, a small sloop of 90 tons.

The ships were outfitted with a cargo of trade items to appeal to the natives in the far corner of the world: blankets, beads, calicos, tin mirrors, brass buttons, earrings, copper kettles, iron chisels, knives, bits of scrap iron and tobacco, both snuff and for smoking. The *Columbia*, under the command of John Kendrick, and the *Washington*, captained by Robert Gray, the second in command, emerged from Boston Harbor on October 1, 1787, squared their sails and set a course to the tip of South America and around Cape Horn. On the way they stopped in the Cape Verde islands and a young negro, Marcus Lopez, was brought aboard.

During the voyage the ships became separated. The *Washington* was the first to reach the North Pacific and she put in at what is believed to be Tillamook Bay. A boat was sent to shore and at first the natives appeared friendly, giving presents of berries and freshly-caught crabs to the crew.

As the party made ready to return to the ship Marcus Lopez remembered he had left his knife sticking in the sand. He went back after it, found it in possession of one of the natives and in attempting to wrestle it away he was killed. In the short battle that followed several Indians were shot with muskets. The landing party retreated, rowed back to the ship and Gray ordered the *Washington* to set sail.

Gray and Kendrick met at Nootka Sound on Vancouver Island. They took turns commanding the *Washington*, running the small ship up and down the coast collecting furs and transferring them to the *Columbia*, which lay at anchor. When the cargo had been secured Gray and Kendrick switched command. Kendrick stayed in the North Pacific with the *Washington* and Gray sailed the *Columbia* to Canton and on to her home port.

The *Columbia*, returning to Boston with a cargo of tea, became the first ship to circle the globe flying the Stars and Stripes. The *Columbia* was outfitted again and on September 28, 1790 departed on her second voyage. Arriving along the North Pacific coast eight months later Gray expected to find Kendrick and the *Washington* waiting. But Kendrick had slipped off to the Sandwich Islands where he was accidently killed by a British vessel when it fired a cannon to salute him.

Gray spent the winter on Vancouver Island, in the harbor of Clayoquot. He built a fort for protection and waited. One day Attoo, the son of a Sandwich Island chief and a member of the crew since the first voyage, came to Gray and told him of a plan of betrayal. He said the natives had promised to make him chief of their tribe if he would smuggle them gunpowder and wet the remaining gunpowder at the fort so it would be useless.

The *Columbia* had been pulled from the water for the winter but Gray ordered her launched and her guns remounted. The natives witnessed this and, knowing they had lost the element of surprise, gave up their plan to attack. Gray sought to punish the natives for their treachery and as they departed in the spring he ordered his men to burn to the ground the nearby native village of 200 houses.

The *Columbia* sailed south, following close to the coastline, and near the 46th parallel Gray recognized the telltale signs of a great river; the darkness of the water and evidence of brush, limbs and trees washed from inland. He searched for the source but could not find it. He returned north, to near the Strait of Juan de Fuca, where the watch called out that a ship was on the horizon. Within a few hours Captain George Vancouver aboard the *Discovery* was within hailing distance.

Vancouver was acting as an agent of the British government, as commander of an expedition sent to survey and map America's northwest coast. He had sailed with Captain Cook on two voyages, one to Antarctica and the other to the North Pacific. He told Gray he had searched for the mythical River of the West and had found no evidence it existed. "Under the most favorable circumstances of wind and weather I have found the whole coast to be one compact and nearly straight barrier against the sea," he said.

Gray volunteered information that he had located a great river at 46° 10', the latitude where Heceta had first made note of it. He had found the bar impassable for the nine days he was there. Vancouver did not believe Gray. He weighed anchor and sailed north into the Strait of Juan de Fuca. Gray lingered a few days and with the weather improving sailed the *Columbia* toward its destiny with discovery.

The morning of May 11, 1792 Gray sailed into the break in the coastline where he had located the river. The water was discolored an inky brown. A strong wind was blowing out of the west and breakers lined the entrance to the river bar. Gray searched for the safest point to cross and at last he gave the order to set sail.

According to his log: "At 8 A.M., being a little to windward of the entrance to the harbor, bore away, and run in east-northeast, between breakers, having from five to seven fathoms of water. When we were over the bar we found this to be a large river of fresh water, up which we steered. Many canoes came alongside.... Vast numbers of natives came alongside. People employed in pumping the salt water out of our water casks, in order to fill with fresh, while the ship floated in. So ends."

John Boit, a member of the crew, wrote in his journal: "We directed our course up this noble River in search of a village. The beach was lin'd with natives, who ran along the shore following the ship. Soon after, above 20 canoes came off, and brought a good lot of furs and

salmon, which last they sold, two for a board Nail. The furs we likewise bought cheap, for Copper and Cloth.... (May 15) We contented ourselves in our present situation, which was a very pleasant one. I landed abreast the ship with Capt. Gray to view the country and take possession. Found much clear ground, fit for cultivation, and the woods mostly clear from underbrush."

On May 20th the *Columbia* attempted to float out to sea on high tide but as it neared the bar the wind failed. Without wind the *Columbia* would drift into the breakers and likely be torn apart. The anchor was dropped and she came up in three and one-half fathoms. Later a fresh wind sprang from the sea and Gray wrote in his log: "At 5 P.M. we were out, clear of all bars, and in twenty fathoms of water. A breeze came from the southward; we bore away to the northward, set all sail to the best advantage."

After naming Columbia's River and claiming it for the United States of America, Gray sailed north to the Queen Charlotte's Isles. There the *Columbia* ran aground on hidden rocks and was nearly lost. But she floated free on the incoming tide. Her crew, laboring on the bilge pumps, kept her afloat and she limped into Nootka Sound and was beached for repairs.

In later years Gray's discovery became the basis for the United States' claim to the Pacific Northwest. It also marked the end of the sea trading era. A new age was beginning as overland explorers pushed into the interior.

Books by Rick Steber

TALES OF THE WILD WEST

A continuing series that celebrates the rich history of the West. Each volume contains 50 short stories. Current titles include: *OREGON TRAIL, PACIFIC COAST, INDIANS, COWBOYS, WOMEN OF THE WEST, CHILDREN'S STORIES, LOGGERS, MOUNTAIN MEN, MINERS, GRANDPA'S STORIES, PIONEER STORIES, CAMPFIRE STORIES.*

OREGON TRAIL— LAST OF THE PIONEERS

Our final link to history's most famous trail is the firsthand accounts of these last living pioneers.

HEARTWOOD

Stories of the men and women who settled the West. A treasure you will want to pass on to your children and grandchildren.

NEW YORK TO NOME—THE NORTHWEST PASSAGE BY CANOE

The true adventure of the 1936-1937 expedition to discover the Northwest Passage.

WILD HORSE RIDER

A biography of the 1912 World Saddlebronc Champion, Lew Minor.